Contents

The Night Before Christmas

and other Christmas Stories

Brown Watson

ENGLAND

The Night Before Christmas

'Twas the night before Christmas,

when all through the house

Not a creature was stirring,

not even a mouse;

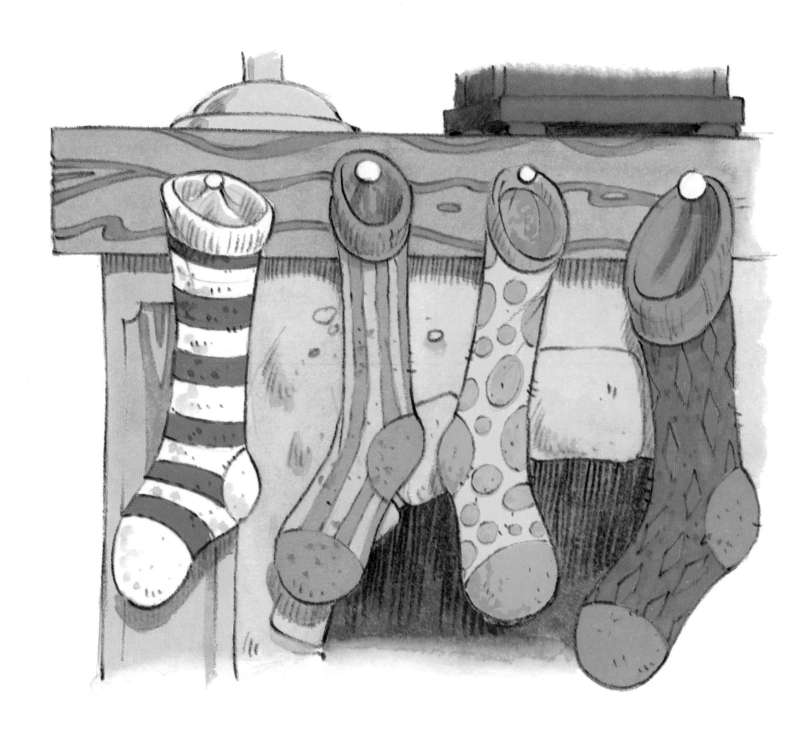

The stockings were hung
        by the chimney with care,
In hopes that St. Nicholas
        soon would be there.

The children were nestled

all snug in their beds,

While visions of sugarplums

danced in their heads;

And mamma in her kerchief,

and I in my cap,

Had just settled our brains

for a long winter nap;

When out on the lawn

there arose such a clatter,

I sprang from my bed

to see what was the matter.

Away to the window

I flew like a flash,

Tore open the shutters

and threw up the sash.

The moon, on the breast

of the new-fallen snow,

Gave a lustre of midday

to objects below,

When, what to my wondering
eyes should appear,
But a miniature sleigh
and eight tiny reindeer,

With a little old driver
   so lively and quick,
I knew in a moment
   it must be St. Nick.

More rapid than eagles,
his coursers they came,
And he whistled and shouted
and called them by name:

"Now, Dasher! now, Dancer!
now, Prancer and Vixen!

'On Comet! on Cupid!
on Donner and Blitzen!
To the top of the porch,
to the top of the wall,

Now, dash away! dash away!

dash away all!"

As dry leaves that before
the wild hurricane fly,
When they meet with an obstacle,
mount to the sky,

So up to the housetop
the coursers they flew,
With the sleigh full of toys,
and St. Nicholas, too.

And then, in a twinkling,

I heard on the roof

The prancing and pawing

of each little hoof.

As I drew in my head,

and was turning around,

Down the chimney St. Nicholas

came with a bound.

He was dressed all in fur

from his head to his foot,

And his clothes were all tarnished

with ashes and soot;

A bundle of toys

he had flung on his back,

And he looked like a pedlar

just opening his pack.

His eyes – how they twinkled!

His dimples – how merry!

His cheeks were like roses,

his nose like a cherry.

His droll little mouth

was drawn up like a bow,

And the beard on his chin

was as white as the snow.

He had a broad face

and a little round belly

That shook when he laughed

like a bowlful of jelly.

He was chubby and plump,

a right jolly old elf,

And I laughed when I saw him

in spite of myself.

A wink of his eye

and a twist of his head

Soon gave me to know

I had nothing to dread.

He spoke not a word,

but went straight to his work,

And filled all the stockings;

then turned with a jerk,

And laying his finger

aside of his nose,

And giving a nod,

up the chimney he rose.

He sprang to his sleigh,

to his team gave a whistle

And away they all flew

like the down of a thistle.

But I heard him exclaim,

'ere he drove out of sight,

"Happy Christmas to all,

and to all a good night!"

Teddy's
Christmas Present

Teddy Bear had lots of nice toys, but his favourite had always been Ernest, the engine.

Teddy loved his big, smiley face and the clickety-clack, clickety-clack of his wheels, as he pulled the train behind him.

Ernest had been Teddy's friend ever since he could remember. But now, the old engine was becoming very battered and worn. More than once, a wheel had come off and Daddy Bear had fixed it back on.

His face had become cracked, his
buffer beam was bent and his
paintwork was scratched. And more
than once, his funnel had come off!
"I don't know how many more times
I can mend Ernest," said Daddy.

"Ernest is getting quite old now, you know," Daddy Bear went on, reaching for his screwdriver. "And you play with him every day, Teddy." "I know," said Teddy sadly. He wondered what he could do.

Just then, Mummy Bear came in, a shopping basket over her arm. "What do you think?" she cried. "Santa Claus is coming to Teddy Town tomorrow, to see what all the teddies want for Christmas!"

"Hear that, Teddy?" smiled Daddy. "You can ask him to bring you a nice, new engine! You've been a good bear all year, so I think Santa Claus would do it."
But Teddy Bear shook his head.

"No," he said, "I don't want a new engine to take the place of Ernest, just because he's old and tired." Then, he thought again. "But I could ask Santa Claus to make him as good as new, couldn't I?"

He sat down to write to Santa Claus that same afternoon, telling him all about Ernest. "I do not want any new toys," he wrote, "but I hope you can make Ernest like new. Please try. Love Teddy."

Santa Claus did not see how he could help. "Toys do get old," he said, stroking his beard. "It's a pity Teddy does not want a new engine. Eric's a nice little one, and he needs a good home . . ."

"I know how Teddy feels," thought Santa. "I only wish I could make old toys into new ones."
Then a sudden movement of snow caught his eye and he looked across towards the stables.

Dasher had been away having his hooves trimmed, all ready for Christmas Eve. Now, he was back with Dancer, and seeing how glad both reindeer were to be together gave Santa Claus an idea!

The teddies of Teddy Town were pleased to see Santa Claus sitting by the big Christmas tree in the market. He soon saw Teddy Bear coming towards him, holding Ernest the engine very tightly.

"So, this is Ernest," he said, making Ernest feel very proud. "Yes, I can see why you love him so much, Teddy." "Can you make him like new again?" asked Teddy.

"Well," said Santa Claus, "I can't make him a new engine on the outside, but I think I can make him a new engine inside, would that do?" Teddy did not really understand this, but he nodded and smiled.

"As long as I don't have a new engine in place of Ernest," he said. "No, Teddy," Santa Claus laughed, reaching in his sack. "But I do have something so that Ernest will be able to rest a little."

It was a lovely, little engine shed! Teddy could hardly wait to take it home and see what Ernest looked like, resting inside.

"Oh, thank you, Santa Claus!" he cried. "Thank you very much!"

Teddy felt rather muddled as he did think that Santa Claus had given him a special, magic sort of present to make Ernest feel like new again. Yet, although he had waited patiently, nothing had happened.

But, Teddy was wrong. Being alone in the engine shed had made Ernest think how nice it would be to have a friend. So, he was very, very pleased when someone in a red cloak and hood put another engine in the shed beside him!

"Hello," whispered the new, little engine with a friendly grin.
"My name is Eric!"
"And I'm Ernest!" whispered Ernest.
"Merry Christmas to both of you!" whispered Santa Claus.

Ernest and Eric talked long into the night, chatting about trains and tracks and rails. It made Ernest feel most important, telling his new friend all about Teddy Bear and the fun they would share.

And what a surprise Teddy had on Christmas morning! It was hard not to like such a bright, cheerful-looking engine, such as Eric – especially when Teddy could see he was already Ernest's friend!

And Ernest? Well, his funnel was still wobbly and his wheels loose but his smile was bright and his paintwork sparkled. It was plain he felt a new engine inside, just as Santa Claus had promised!

And, as Ernest watched Eric pulling
the trucks, Teddy could see that he
did not mind having a rest. And
how much nicer the shed looked
with two engines to go inside!
Clever old Santa Claus!

Snowy
The Christmas Snowman

"Cold enough for snow!" said Simon and Julie's dad, taking one last look out at their back garden before locking the door for the night.

"I hope not!" said Mum, who was busy baking. "I hate Christmas shopping when it snows."

All the same, Simon and Julie couldn't help wishing that it WOULD snow – even if it was just enough to build a snowman for Christmas! And when they woke up next day – what do you think?

Roofs of houses and garden sheds, window sills, fences and lawns were powdered with snow, sparkling in the winter sunshine like icing sugar. "Great!" Simon cried. "We can build a snowman."

"You'll have to be quick!" laughed
Dad. "We didn't have much snow,
and it won't last long."
"Good!" said Mum, mixing the cake.
"I'm glad," added Gran.

The children put on their coats, wellingtons, woolly hats and gloves and went outside. "It's true what Dad says," sighed Julie looking around. "There isn't really all that much snow . . ."

"I think there's enough by the wall," Simon told her, scooping up quite a few handfuls. "See if you can make a big snowball for the head, and I'll start on the snowman's body."

Julie found that getting enough snow to make even a little snowball was not easy. Scraping the whole of the garden fence only gave her a tiny handful, and most of that was already melting.

Simon had not done much better with the snowman's body. And if Mum hadn't opened an upstairs window, sending down a shower of snow, they would never have managed to finish him, at all.

"He's a bit small . . ." said Julie. "Don't worry!" said Simon. "We can always make him bigger, as long as we get some more snow before Christmas. Let's call him Snowy, the Christmas Snowman!"

The weather stayed quite cold, but there was no more snow.

"At least I can hang out some washing," said Mum.

"And I can do some Christmas shopping," smiled Gran.

Julie and Simon were both very disappointed.
"Oh, please don't worry about your snowman," Dad told them. "That wall gets hardly any sun, you know. He'll last until Christmas."

But there was no mistake about it. Snowy was getting smaller and smaller. And the smaller he got, the easier it became for the pale, winter sun to melt more and more of him away.

If it had not been for Jack Frost coming round every night and touching everything with his long, icy fingers, Snowy knew he would never have lasted so long.

Everyone else seemed so happy. Fairy lights appeared in all the windows, and Snowy could hear Simon and Julie laughing and chatting as they helped to put up the decorations.

"It's time to mix the Christmas pudding!" came Mum's voice. "Take it in turns to make a wish!"
"I'd wish to be a real Christmas snowman!" thought Snowy.

Snowy glanced up at the dark sky, hoping he'd see clouds gathering around. Instead, it was a clear night, with lots of stars.

He saw something gliding towards the moon, and a man in a red suit. It was pulled by animals with what looked like tree branches on their heads . . .

"Reindeer . . ." whispered Snowy. Simon and Julie had talked a lot about Santa Claus and what they hoped he would bring them on his sleigh. Snowy knew he came from a land of ice and snow . . .

"I wish Santa Claus could bring me some snow," thought poor Snowy. He closed his eyes tight, not wanting to see anything to remind him of the happy time Christmas was meant to be.

At first, Snowy thought he was dreaming. Something soft began falling on his face, his head, then his body, fluttering all around him like a shower of bright moonbeams, making him feel warm and happy.

"Snow!" cried Snowy joyfully.
"Merry Christmas!" came the cry
from above. "Merry Christmas,
Snowy!" And in a final burst of stars
and moonbeams, both reindeer
and sleigh were gone.

"Well, I got just what I wanted for Christmas," said Dad in his new dressing gown. "So did we!" cried Julie and Simon. "Except for our Christmas snowman," added Julie solemnly.

"Well," said Grandma, standing at the back door, "I don't know about that. See for yourselves, you two!" Simon and Julie looked at each other, sure that there had been no snow at all.

Snowy, the Christmas snowman stood proud and tall. His head was round and jolly, and his body so plump and cuddly that Julie could not help giving him a hug for Christmas morning.

"Where did the snow come from?" they wondered. "And why isn't there snow anywhere else?" When Julie said that it might have something to do with Santa Claus, how they all laughed!

Santa's Little Helper

It was always cold where Peter lived. All the ice and snow and the green fir trees made everywhere look Christmassy, too – especially when Peter and his dad came back from town on the sledge!

The sledge was always loaded up when Christmas was coming. Not with toys and presents, but with food, clothes and everything else Peter's family needed. A team of dogs pulled it across the snow.

Peter loved all the dogs and helped to look after each one. His favourite was Marcus, the leader. "Daddy," Peter said one day, "why does Santa Claus have reindeer to pull his sleigh?"

"Because he's always had reindeer, I suppose," smiled Daddy. "I just happen to like dogs best."

"So do I!" said Peter. "Marcus could pull the sleigh across the sky without any trouble."

Peter went indoors to write his Christmas letter. What he wanted more than anything else was a guitar. "My Daddy could teach me how to play it," he wrote, "and everyone would enjoy the music."

Peter finished by writing about his clever dog, Marcus. But he was wondering if Father Christmas really could bring the guitar he wanted so badly. He had only ever seen a picture of one, in a book.

An icy blast of wind lifted Peter's letter up and up into the dark, wintry sky, until it was like a big snowflake, whirling round and round. Then, at last, it floated down on a cloud.

At least, it looked like a cloud to anyone who might have been watching. But really, it was a heap of letters. "We'll never get all these sorted out!" someone cried. "It's Christmas Eve, soon!"

"We'll manage!" came a jolly-sounding voice – and a big chubby hand in a red sleeve picked up Peter's letter. "How many times have I said that Christmas comes but once a year?"

But even Santa Claus had to admit that he and his workshops did seem to be extra busy! There was so much to do! Toys to be sorted out, presents wrapped and loaded on to his sleigh . . . .

"Mind out, Prancer!" puffed Santa Claus, helping to drag a big sack of toys across the snow. "Ooh, I'll be glad to get this lot on the sleigh Then I think we'll have a nice cup of tea . . . ."

Poor Santa! His hands were so cold that the edge of the sack slipped from his fingers.
Teddy Bears, footballs, cars, games . . . . out they all tumbled, rolling around on the snow!

Poor Prancer! He stepped back on a big, toy engine – and down he went, too!

"Prancer!" cried Santa Claus in alarm. "Prancer, are you all right?"

"No Christmas Eve duties for you, boy!" said Santa Claus seeing his hurt leg. Prancer was very upset. And Santa knew the other reindeer could not pull a heavy sleigh without him . . . .

All was quiet that Christmas Eve. Everyone had been working hard. Now all that could be heard was the rustle of coal as it shifted on the fire and the whisper of snow against the window.

Peter was fast asleep, dreaming of everyone singing and dancing to his guitar, just as he had told Santa Claus. He did not hear a low whistle outside in the snow. But someone else did . . . .

"Here, Marcus, old boy!" called Santa Claus, as the dog appeared. "Peter told me all about you. Would you like to help pull my sleigh?" Marcus wagged his tail without stopping.

Santa Claus put on the jangly harness, just like Peter fastened the straps when Marcus pulled the sledge. But, as soon as he stepped out with the reindeer – can you guess what happened?

The sleigh lifted up into the sky, stars twinkling all around! "Get some speed up!" cried Santa Claus, shaking the reins with a merry, jingling sound. "Lots to do before Christmas morning!"

And so there was. Hundreds of chimney stacks, thousands of roofs, across towns and big cities, farms and villages! Santa Claus and his sleigh visited them all. Marcus had never seen such sights!

Dawn was just beginning to break as Santa Claus steered the sleigh back to Peter's home. "Thanks for your help, Marcus!" he said, giving him a pat. "We'd never have managed without you!"

Peter got up early next morning. "Do you know," he said very sleepily, "I had a lovely dream last night. It was all about Marcus going with Santa Claus, helping the reindeer to pull his sleigh!"

"You were asking me if I thought Marcus could do the job," Daddy smiled. "So maybe you went to bed wondering about it. Anyway, come and see what Santa Claus has left for you."

There were sweets, toys – and a big parcel with a label tied on it.
"DEAR PETER," it read, "HERE IS A SPECIAL PRESENT FOR TELLING ME ABOUT YOUR DOG, MARCUS. HE WAS A GREAT HELP TO ME AND MY REINDEER!"
Peter did not know which he